"" The sea seemed to boil around the boat, frothing red as a fin broke the surface. Suddenly the shark's head rose above water. Jaws clamped on the diver's leg – his wetsuit ripped open.

The diver screamed before plunging down to the seabed again, the shark dragging him by his ankle. Taylor could only stare in horror at the churning frenzy under his boat and the helpless man struggling in a swirl of blood. ""

Dead in the Water
by John Townsend

Published by Ransom Publishing Ltd.
Unit 7, Brocklands Farm, West Meon, Hampshire
GU32 1JN, UK
www.ransom.co.uk

ISBN   978 178127 946 5
First published in 2015

BREAKOUTS

DEAD
IN THE WATER

John Townsend

Ransom

4

Erskine Library
Bridgewater Place, Erskine, PA8 7AA
Renfrewshire Libraries, TEL: 0300 300 1188

Customer ID: *****0603

Items that you have checked out

Title: Dead in the water
ID: 195822121
Due: 13 June 2023

Total items: 1
Checked out: 1
Overdue: 0
Hold requests: 0
Ready for collection: 0
16/05/2023 19:25

Thank you for using the bibliotheca SelfCheck System.

ONE

A beach in Australia

A dark fin sliced through the waves. It swerved one way, then another, before heading straight towards the beach. Close to shore, it swerved again in a wide arc before dipping below the water.

The last of the body-boarders still surfed the breakers as a red sun slowly sank over the sea. By now, few people remained on the beach and the lifeguards had already gone. Their hut was locked and empty – beside the swaying sign squeaking in the warm sea breeze that said: BEWARE SHARKS.

A tailfin broke the surface with a hiss of spray as it thrashed through the shallows. With two more sweeps of its powerful tail, the huge fish sped over a sand bank and along the shoreline. Its striped body rose and its back skimmed silently through the rolling waves. At first no one heard or saw the shadow moving along the seabed … closing in on human prey.

Tyler pulled on the oars as his dinghy rode the swell of another large wave. 'I'm starving. Shall we head for home?'

His two passengers laughed.

'How can you eat so much and keep so skinny?' Maddie sat back and trailed her hand in the water. 'Row us ashore and we can cook Blake's fish on a barbie.'

Blake didn't take his eyes off his fishing line. 'I'll try to catch another one first. We need to fatten Tyler up, or he'll never grow.'

'I happen to be super-fit and just burn up loads of

energy, that's all!' Tyler purposely splashed them with a sweep of an oar. 'Don't forget, I'm "Twelve-year-old Swimming Champ of White Reef Bay." ' He looked directly at Maddie. 'Blake's just jealous of his fit little brother.'

'I reckon I was far fitter than you a couple of years back, when I was your age,' Blake grunted as he cast his fishing line once more.

'What was that?' Maddie stared into the water. 'Did you see it?'

'Yeah, yeah – you're always seeing stuff. Maybe it's a mermaid trying to hitch a ride.' Blake spoke without taking his eyes from his fishing rod.

'I think I saw something too, Maddie,' Tyler said softly – with an edge of concern. He stopped rowing and stood up gingerly. 'There's something really dark moving over the seabed.'

All three of them peered over the side at a blurry shape moving below them.

7

'Don't tip us over!' Tyler shouted, as the boat suddenly dipped to one side.

'It's only a scuba diver down there,' Blake said. 'No wonder I haven't caught anything if he's scared off all the fish. Look, you can see his bubbles coming up just over ... '

Before he could finish speaking, the shark struck.

The sea seemed to boil around the boat, frothing red as a fin broke the surface. Suddenly the shark's head rose above water, just metres from Blake's fishing line. Jaws clamped on the diver's leg – his wetsuit ripped open. He screamed before plunging down to the seabed again, the shark dragging him by his ankle. Tyler could only stare in horror at the churning frenzy under his boat and the helpless man struggling in a swirl of blood.

Blake shouted. 'Keep still. Don't move. It's a dirty great tiger shark.'

Maddie squealed. 'But that poor diver guy – can't we do something?'

'That brute could smash my dinghy to bits. If it comes up again, I'll bash it with the paddle.' Tyler lifted an oar, desperate not to rock the boat. In the long silence that followed, the water cleared beneath them and all fell deathly still.

All of a sudden a cry came from behind them. 'Help me!'

They looked round to see the diver's head above water. 'Help me – shark!'

He tried to swim towards them as a dorsal fin broke the surface just metres behind him. Tyler swung the oar towards the diver's grasping hands.

Maddie shouted frantically, 'Hurry – it's coming back – behind you!'

Blake grabbed the other oar. 'Get on the other side,

Maddie. I'm gonna reach over, but don't let this boat tip or we'll all be DITW.'

Maddie frowned till Tyler explained. '*Dead In The Water*. Whatever you do, don't fall out of this thing, Maddie.' He stretched his arm and leaned out as far as he could reach. The diver made a lunge for the oar and grabbed hold, as the fin swerved past before circling the boat.

'It's about to attack!' Blake shouted. 'It's gonna ram us.'

While Tyler tried to pull the diver towards them, Blake splashed the paddle on the other side, slapping the water. The vibrations brought the shark rushing up from far below – its jaws wide open. With one splintering crunch, it bit Blake's oar in two. Maddie snatched his fish-knife and threw it at the shark's snout. The blade struck like a harpoon.

The shark immediately dived again, giving Tyler and Blake just enough time to haul the diver into the boat.

He fell inside, panting and groaning. They could see he was in a bad way and tried to stop the bleeding. Tyler tore off his T shirt to tie around the man's gaping leg. Maddie was already on her phone calling for help, while Blake kept repeating, 'It's OK, mate – you're safe now.'

But they all knew he wasn't safe – and nor were they. They could only watch helplessly as the shark's fin swept around them again and again. Twice it slammed into the boat and drenched them. Maddie fell backwards but clung on as the boat spun and rocked violently.

Suddenly the huge fin turned away and headed out to sea. Fearing the shark would turn back and charge, Tyler began rowing to shore as fast as he could. Soon they were carried onto the beach in the surf. At least they were now safe from the shark's razor teeth, but Tyler knew that the next minutes would be a frantic race. A race between life and death.

TWO

Blake and Tyler dragged the boat up the beach while Maddie ran to warn surfers nearby. No one had seen the attack, so all were happily diving through the waves, unaware of danger.

'There's a tiger shark out there. It's just attacked a guy!' she shouted above the thundering of breaking waves. A woman locking up a drinks kiosk stared at her frostily.

'Don't scare people with your sick jokes. We've surfed

here for years – it's the safest beach for miles. I'm not having my business wrecked by you telling crazy scare stories.' Her stony face had a mean stare, a gold lip-ring and a pearl tongue-stud. Her cropped, bleached hair was as spiky as her manner.

Maddie was lost for words. 'Look – I've got proof,' she said, showing a picture on her phone. 'I took this just now. You can see its jaws snapping the paddle in half. The guy back there in the boat nearly lost his leg. We've got to get him to hospital.'

The woman glared angrily. 'I never listen to kids. You make up all this stuff. And don't let me hear you say any more about sharks round here. Get off this beach and go home.'

She turned and walked away towards the sand dunes. Maddie was stunned. How could anyone be like that? But before she had chance to say anything, a helicopter appeared overhead. The air ambulance had arrived.

✳

Inside his boat, Tyler continued to tighten bandages around the diver's leg. Blood was still seeping where the flesh was torn open, from ankle to knee. Blake tried to keep the man talking.

'You'll be OK. The paramedics are here. The air ambulance is just landing.'

He shielded the man's face from the swirling sand thrown up by the helicopter's rotor blades. Suddenly the man gripped Blake's arm and mumbled, 'Tell her 559620. Tell her. Get the camera. It's proof. Have you got that number? 559620.'

Blake repeated it. 'Yeah, don't you worry. 559620.'

The man gasped and closed his eyes before adding, 'Tell Liz. Warn her. You *must* warn her of Kirk. Stop them.' He loosened his grip on Blake's arm and sighed as his head flopped to one side. By the time the paramedics arrived, he wasn't moving … or breathing.

Tyler flopped in front of the TV. He was exhausted. Police and reporters had questioned him for hours. He tapped the remote and called, 'Hey – Blake. It's the news. We might be on it.'

Blake joined him on the sofa just as the newsreader made a dramatic announcement: 'News just in. A diver has been attacked by a large tiger shark in White Reef Bay, only metres from the beach. He has been named as Professor Brian Hill, a local marine zoologist. He suffered major injuries and had to be revived by medics at the scene. They rushed him to hospital, where he is said to be in a critical condition. The medics said Professor Hill wouldn't have survived at all if three children hadn't rescued him from the sea and given first aid. They raised the alarm and an air ambulance was on the scene in minutes. Our reporter has spoken to the three young people concerned ... '

'So the guy was a prof,' Blake said. 'I really hope they can save him.'

'*Ssh*, this is us.' Tyler turned up the sound.

The reporter they'd spoken to earlier appeared on the screen. She stood on the beach with the moon behind her and spoke with urgency over the pounding waves: 'This is the spot where the attack took place, earlier today. First to act swiftly was Tyler, who was rowing his brother and twelve-year-old cousin, Maddie. He describes what he saw … '

Tyler stared in disbelief as his face filled the screen and he heard himself saying, 'The first thing I knew something was wrong was when a diver swam under my boat and a big shark grabbed him. It looked like it was biting off the man's leg, but I reckon he somehow pulled away and swam up and grabbed my paddle. We pulled him in the boat just as the shark rammed us a few times. I managed to row us to shore, where we looked after him till help arrived.'

'You make it all sound easy. Weren't you scared?'

'Yeah – I guess. But you just have to do what you can. Maddie's got a picture of the shark. It's awesome.'

Maddie's phone image appeared on the screen with her voice describing it: 'When it rammed the boat I fell backwards and nearly dropped my phone in the sea. But it was cool to fight it off and rescue the diver.'

Blake appeared on the screen next, looking straight into the camera. 'I have to say my kid brother is the hero. He got the guy out the sea and bandaged him up. I've never seen him row so fast!'

The reporter asked another question. 'Tell us about Professor Hill's injuries.'

Blake paused before telling the world, 'Pretty bad. The poor guy was in pain and mumbling a lot. I think he passed out a couple of times.'

'What was he able to tell you?'

'Just random stuff. He was a bit dazed so it didn't make much sense. He told me a number and something about a camera and proof and stuff. He gave me a couple of names but that's about it.'

Blake's image faded from the screen as the reporter gave figures about recent shark attacks around Australia.

The woman with the gold lip-ring swore at the TV and snatched her phone. She shouted into it and swore again. 'You messed it up. Have you seen the news? Those kids know something. Get them.'

THREE

The police called to see Blake and Tyler the next morning.

'Someone has asked to see you. She saw you on the news last night and wants to ask you a couple of questions. It's up to you – you don't have to see her if you don't want to. She works at the university with Professor Hill. We've checked her out and she's a good friend of his. Her name is Liz Bevan. She's a marine zoologist.'

Blake already knew his answer. 'Yeah – sure. I'll talk to her if it helps. Prof Hill told me to tell someone called Liz … to warn her about a guy called Kirk. I've got no idea what he was saying but I may as well tell her. Any news of how the prof is getting on?'

'They're still fighting to save him. He's on a life-support machine. They've given him a lot of blood and the doctors hope to wake him when they've finished stitching him up.'

✳

Liz Bevan sat at her desk, surrounded by computer screens. 'I'm so glad you came to see me,' she told Blake. 'You're my hero for what you've done for Brian. I want you to know what a great guy he is. The work we're doing here is so important to us and the thing is … ' She paused to choose her words.

'The thing is, we know there are people who want to stop us. We have to work in secret, which is why I need your help. I won't bore you with all the details of our research, but a lot of it involves trying to protect the coral reef. Coral is a real wonder of science and home to such a range of sea life, but it's under great threat – and not just from pollution and climate change. There are coral thieves who keep hacking great chunks of it to sell. Coral is an ancient living ecosystem and of huge importance to our planet.'

'Is that where the prof was diving yesterday?' Blake asked.

'Yes. Just close to the reef is our star creature. Brian is studying a giant clam that's many years old and has the biggest, most perfect pearl we've ever seen. It would fetch millions of dollars if the thieves got hold of it. So, you see, it's vital we protect these living treasures just out there.'

She pointed at a smashed door. 'Thieves broke in the other night. They cracked Brian's safe and stole his map of the reef to find out where the clam is. Luckily he's never written down the exact details. Even *I* don't know the map reference. That's how secret we have to be.'

The young woman sighed and looked into Blake's eyes. 'When I saw you on the news last night, I sensed you're an honest young guy who I can trust. I need to ask you a straight question.'

'Go right ahead.'

'Have you got Brian's camera?'

'No. I never saw it.'

Liz looked away and added bluntly, 'I would pay you a lot for it. Name your price.'

Blake snapped back, 'I told you the truth. I never saw his camera. And if I had it, I'd give it to the police.'

Liz smiled. 'OK. Sorry I had to ask, but I can never be sure who can be trusted. You pass my test with flying colours! I can tell you're one of the good guys. I guess I can tell you this – but keep it to yourself. You see, Brian was filming evidence yesterday. His camera hasn't just got images of Pamela, but also images of the coral thieves in action.'

Blake frowned, 'Who's Pamela?'

'Sorry,' she laughed. 'Pamela is our clam. *Pam the Clam*. Brian found a little tunnel in the reef that he could squeeze into and film the thieves unseen. Look at his last blog entry from yesterday … ' She clicked on his webpage and his blog appeared on her screen:

Pirates of our Ocean Habitat

I am getting evidence of the criminals. I am about to reveal their names so they can be arrested. We need to **SAVE OUR SEAS** before it is too late …

Liz turned to Blake and spoke with tears in her eyes. 'Brian always took an undersea phone on his dives. He called me just before the shark attacked. His last message to me was that he'd caught the thieves on film and he was bringing it back as proof, so we could identify them and get them locked up.'

Blake shook his head. 'He didn't have his camera when we found him. It must have dropped to the seabed – or was swallowed by the shark. You won't get it back now.' He took a scrap of paper from his pocket. 'I wrote down a number the prof told me. He asked me to tell "Liz" this number – so I guess it's for you.' He put it on the desk.

'I've got no idea what this means,' she said. '559620 means nothing at all. Did Brian say any more?'

'There was something else,' Blake said thoughtfully. 'It's probably just another random thing he gabbled in pain. He told me to warn you about someone called Kirk.'

Liz stared without speaking. After a long pause she repeated, 'Kirk?'

'I'm pretty sure that's what he told me,' Blake said, beginning to doubt himself. 'Maybe I got it wrong if that name doesn't mean anything.'

'It means something, all right. I know of Dr Kirk. He runs a project at the Sea Life Centre. It's a bit of a crazy project, too. I happen to think it's a silly gimmick just to bring in tourists and get big funding. It's called *The Megalodon Show*.'

Blake's eyebrows rose in surprise. 'Wow – mega sharks. I've read about them. Megalodon sharks used to swim round here. They were at least 20 metres long. They'd make great white sharks look like sardines. I'm glad they're extinct!'

'According to Kirk they're not! He reckons a few are still out there. He's found huge teeth and says they're not as old as scientists first thought. Brian calls Kirk *Doctor Shark*, not just because he studies them but because he's always circling round us, hoping to grab bits of our research and gulp down any funding he can get! Apart from that, he seems pretty harmless.'

Blake's phone bleeped. 'Hey, it's my kid brother. He and Maddie are on the beach.'

'I'd like to meet them,' Liz said.

'You can come with me,' Blake suggested, as he put his phone down. 'Tyler says I need to get over there. They've found something washed up on the sand.'

'Was it the camera?'

'He wouldn't say, but I guess it must be important.'

FOUR

Tyler stood barefoot on the sand and stared out to sea. Rumbling waves tumbled onto the beach before sweeping around his feet.

'I'm just wondering what creatures are out there,' he said. 'That ocean hides so many secrets.'

'I can't believe people are still surfing,' Maddie added. 'They must be mad after we warned them. I just hope that tiger shark doesn't come back.'

'Even the lifeguards are out there – look at them posing as always.' He pointed at two men on jet skis racing over the sea. Suddenly a hand gripped his shoulder. He turned to face Blake.

'Don't look so scared, it's only me!' Blake grinned. 'This is Liz who works with the prof. She wants to meet you.'

'I need to thank you,' Liz began. 'You saved Brian's life. If he makes it, we've got you to thank. Blake said you'd found something. It wouldn't be a camera, would it?'

'Down there,' Maddie pointed. It's half the oar from Tyler's boat. It got washed up here. You can see all the teeth marks and there's a big tooth stuck in it. It's really sharp and jagged. At least it's proof we didn't make it up. The woman at the kiosk didn't want to believe me. She called me a liar.'

'I'm going to put that oar on display,' Tyler announced proudly. 'I want to keep it forever.'

Liz looked disappointed. 'I was hoping someone had found Brian's camera. It's got important stuff recorded on it.'

'It'll be at the bottom of the sea where the shark got him,' Tyler said. 'But I can't tell you the exact place. It's hard to tell from here.'

'I know!' Maddie waved her phone at them. 'I can tell the exact place. I've got a GPS app on my phone. It tells me exactly where I took the last picture – the one of the shark. Look ... those numbers tell you the grid reference.'

Liz's face lit up. 'That's terrific. I can use that to show me where to dive and get the camera back.'

Tyler was shocked. 'But what if that tiger shark is still out there?'

Liz smiled. 'They say lightning never strikes in the same place twice.'

'That's not really true,' Tyler frowned. 'Besides, a shark is nothing like lightning. It can strike wherever it wants.'

'I'll take the risk,' she said. 'Any chance of using your little boat? I'd like to try.'

'I'll come with you,' Blake said. 'I'll row if you like. How about it, Tyler?'

'I've only just finished cleaning it,' Tyler answered. 'It was in a mess after yesterday. I found this thing inside it. Was it the professor's?' He took from his pocket a silver disc, like a large coin with a clip on it.

Liz nodded. 'That's a mini-transmitter, like the one Brian wore strapped to his ankle. It's called a *Shark Shifter*. It's meant to keep sharks away by giving a signal to scare them off, but clearly it didn't work.'

Before Liz had chance to examine it, the sound of engines grew louder and closer. Two jet skis shot towards them in a shower of spray, before sliding over the wet sand and gliding to a halt beside them. One of the lifeguards lifted his sun goggles onto his head and raised his hand.

'Hi guys. Fancy a ride on the back?'

Tyler's response was instant. 'Wow – you bet!'

The two sleek machines purred and shone in the sunlight. One was sparkling red with silver stripes and the other was shimmering blue with gold. One had fiery letters streaking along its side: 'DOOM ANGEL' and the other a stylish 'MOON GLADE' glinting across its glossy body.

'I can see you're impressed,' one of the men winked. They both sat astride their jet skis in only their shorts. Each of them was tanned, muscular and stubble-faced. 'I'm Riki. I guess it was you guys we saw on TV last night.'

He had a tattoo of a mermaid on his right shoulder.

'What you did was awesome.' The other man said, giving a salute. 'I'm Jez and I'm glad to meet you.' He shook each of them by the hand.

Maddie wasn't impressed by his gelled hair and greasier charm. 'Why were you out there when you know there's a tiger shark around?' she asked.

'Sharks keep well away from jet skis,' Riki laughed. 'No shark would dare take on us two. We're Supermen!'

'I had to learn the hard way,' Jez added, lifting his leg and showing a long scar along his calf. 'This little beauty was from a great white when I was a kid. Sixty stitches it took to patch me up again. I'm always careful when I swim now. It's a real shame that professor guy didn't take more care. He should have worn a Shark Shifter.'

'He did!' Tyler held up the transmitter.

'That's no good,' Jez sneered. 'It's just cheap and daggy. Mine's top of the range.' He lifted his out of the jet ski. 'This sort never fails. No shark will come within ten metres of this. Not even a megalodon!'

'Prove it!' Blake said. 'Help Liz find something on the seabed.'

Liz butted in, 'Maddie can show us exactly where the camera is. It's got vital info on it. Can you help?'

'What do you reckon, Jez?' Riki smiled a flash of perfect white teeth.

'I guess we could show them how diving can be done properly,' Jez laughed.

Maddie shuddered at the way he laughed. She was the only one to notice the quick look that passed between the two men. A look she didn't like.

'You two must know Dr Kirk,' Liz said. 'Seeing as you mentioned a megalodon. Are those his jet skis by any chance?'

'No idea who you mean,' Jez blurted.

'We got these with our own cash,' Riki laughed.

It was another laugh that made Maddie shudder. It seemed a fake laugh – as if they were lying. Once more she caught a quick look that flashed between them. A look that was nothing less than sinister.

FIVE

A purple speedboat skimmed over the waves in a mist of sea-spray. Jez waved and it swerved towards them, before slowing a short distance offshore. He cheered, 'Hey, a friend of ours has shown up. How would you guys like a spin in that smart new boat? We could whiz you over to it on our jet skis. Then we can go to where you want us to dive. We'll get your camera back in no time.'

Tyler stared, open-mouthed. 'Magic!'

'Thank you so much,' Liz said. 'I'm very grateful.'

'Sounds good to me,' Blake chipped in – but it was Maddie who wasn't so sure.

'I don't think we should,' she said. 'I don't think it's safe.'

'Don't you worry.' Riki smiled and placed his hand on her shoulder. 'We won't let any sharks get you, darling. We'll protect you.'

His words didn't make her feel better. He seemed too creepy for her liking.

'Let's take the older ones first,' Jez said. 'Liz can go with Riki, and Blake can come with me.'

Within seconds the two jet skis zoomed off towards the waiting speedboat.

'Wow – just look at them go,' Tyler gasped. 'I can't wait for my turn!'

Maddie took a photo on her phone. '*I* can. I don't trust them. For a start, how do they know our names? We didn't tell them.'

'You're forgetting something, Maddie,' Tyler grinned. 'We've been on TV. We're famous now.'

✳

As they clambered from the jet skis into the waiting speedboat, Liz reached for her phone. She read a text while Blake turned to watch the jet skis head back to the beach.

The driver of the boat snapped at them. 'Sit down and strap yourselves in. We do things my way from now on.' She glared at them with a hard stare as the sunlight glinted on her gold lip-ring.

Liz didn't look at the woman. She was too busy reading her text message. 'It's from Brian,' she squealed. 'He's sitting up in bed!'

Blake was still staring at the jet skis. 'Hey, that's great news,' he said. 'But there's something I'm a bit puzzled about … '

Before he could tell her, Liz gasped as she read the rest of her text. 'I don't believe it. Brian says he knows who the coral thieves are. When he filmed them diving, they wore shorts and snorkels but showed clear ID. One had a long scar up his leg and the other a mermaid tattoo on his shoulder.'

Blake turned to look at her. 'This is a trap, Liz. The prof warned me about Kirk, and those two guys do know him. You were right – the jet skis must be Kirk's. I've just worked it out. Both 'DOOM ANGEL' and 'MOON GLADE' have the same letters. If you rearrange them, they both spell 'MEGALODON'. Dr Shark is behind this. Something weird is going on … '

Before he could say more, an oar cracked down on him with a thud – and he crumpled into the boat.

*

As a jet ski circled the speedboat at full speed many times, Tyler yelled with delight. He assumed Jez was giving him an extra ride – but there was a more sinister reason. It was to distract Maddie, who'd already sensed that something was wrong. She had to be bundled onto the boat first and tied up with the others. Then their phones were thrown overboard.

When Tyler staggered aboard he was so dizzy it was easy to throw him to the floor and gag him. The engine roared to life and the speedboat leapt from the water. In a purple blur it shot across the waves and headed out to sea, before turning to zoom along the coast to the Sea Life Centre.

The woman behind the wheel smiled for the first time. 'We've got them!'

SIX

Doctor Kirk's bulging waist and unusually puffy neck wobbled when he spoke. 'Welcome to my Sea Life Centre. It's a great place … to die.'

He sat at a shark-shaped desk in the middle of what looked like a massive warehouse with glass walls – the sides of vast fish tanks. 'Fish food costs a fortune,' he smirked. 'That's why I have to feed my enemies to these carnivorous beauties. My megalodon has a wicked taste for human flesh.' He wheezed a sinister chuckle.

'Yes, you heard me correctly. If you look at the far tank you'll see my pride and joy. By injecting growth drugs into great white sharks and using DNA from megalodon teeth, I am cloning the largest fish to swim the seas.'

He leaned back proudly, draped in his super-sized shark-print bath robe.

'Of course it's a big secret till I reveal it to the world and make my fortune. In the meantime, I have to raid the reef and sell coral around the world. But now I must get my hands on Professor Hill's pearl. That's where you will help … '

His four prisoners, now strapped to bars in a low cage at his feet, stared up at the huge shark moving around its tank. The woman with the gold lip-ring stood guard beside them, holding a harpoon gun and sneering. Jez and Riki sat nearby, looking very pleased with themselves.

It was Liz who dared to speak. 'I thought you worked on antidotes to the deadly venom of sea creatures.'

41

'That's my cover. Drug companies pay me for that, but it's just a sideline. The tank behind you is full of the most toxic sea life in the world – from box jelly fish and blue-ringed octopus to sea snakes and stonefish. There's enough deadly venom in that one tank to kill you all fifty times over.'

'What's this got to do with us?' Maddie mumbled. The woman guarding them kicked the cage and shouted, 'Shut it!'

'I brought you here for three reasons,' Doctor Kirk went on. 'First, as punishment. You wrecked my plan. Brian Hill was meant to die and you saved him. He had proof my two friends here were "Seabed Pirates", as he called them. So I had to stop him reporting them. My tiger shark was sent to silence him. It failed because of you. I never accept failure – and I never forgive it.'

He paused and stared at each of them in turn before continuing.

'Second, you planned to find his camera and hand in the evidence. You had to be stopped.'

'And they were,' the woman butted in. 'I succeeded. But now they know too much.'

Kirk ignored her and went on. 'Third, at least one of you has information I need. I want map data of where the rare clam is. I *must* have that giant pearl.'

He thumped the desk and looked at the female guard. 'Zara here is mad about pearls. I promised her a pearl for each of you, once she's fed you to my sharks.'

He wheezed again before waddling over to the largest tank. 'Believe it or not, I swim with the deadliest sharks. I train them with mini transmitters. They learn to respond to different signals – often from miles away. When we broke into Brian Hill's study, we swapped his Shark Shifter with another transmitter. Instead of scaring sharks away, it now signalled "come and eat me". All very simple. It's all to do with rhythms, electronic fields and the shark's fine-tuned receptors all over its body.'

'I can't believe you actually swim with that great mega-thing,' Tyler gasped.

Doctor Kirk's eyes narrowed. 'No one calls me a liar. I shall prove my clever science. You'll see I'm a genius. Alas, it will end with you being eaten alive.'

He snapped his fingers. 'String him up over the tank.'

The two men opened the cage and dragged Tyler towards the shark. Blake shouted, 'Leave my brother. He's done nothing wrong!'

Kirk snarled, 'You said on the TV news that Hill told you a number. What was it?'

Blake paused. 'I can't remember.'

'Then maybe seeing your brother hanging over the

shark tank will help you. That number could be the map reference I need. And don't try giving me false data as I will know by examining the map.'

While Tyler dangled upside down above the water, the enormous shark swam just below his horrified eyes. Blake shook with panic, ripping his hand free from its strap – just as Doctor Kirk climbed the steps up to the tank.

'You will see I have a transmitter on my ankle. It sends a signal to the megalodon not to attack. But when I get out of the water, there will be no signal. As soon as the boy is lowered into the water, it will devour him in an instant.'

Doctor Kirk removed his bath towel and plunged into the tank. In his wetsuit he looked like a blubbery walrus bobbing on the water. The giant shark took no notice of him – even as he swam past its nose.

Tyler wriggled nervously above the tank, swinging by his ankles. He looked down on the fearsome fish and watched Doctor Kirk swimming back-crawl.

'Now that I have proved my point, lower the boy into the tank.'

'No,' Blake blurted. 'I'll tell you the number. I think I know it. It's 5 … 59 … 62 … '

Before he could finish, Tyler shook his whole body. No one heard the plop as a disc fell from his pocket into the tank. As soon as it hit the water, the giant shark lunged forward as if zapped by an electric shock. It thrashed round the tank in a wild frenzy, before opening its jaws. Doctor Kirk screamed as the shark's teeth tore into his blubbery flesh. The water bubbled and turned red.

'Get him out!' Zara yelled, as she and the two men ran to the tank. Blake quickly untied the others and hissed, 'Run for it.'

He darted towards Tyler but stopped when he saw the harpoon gun pointing straight at him. Zara swore and pulled the trigger. The gun fired as Blake dived for cover. A harpoon flew over his head and smashed into the tank behind him. In an instant the glass shattered and a huge wave burst out above his head. It gushed to the floor in front of him, where Zara screamed as a wall of water hit her with full force. A blue-ringed octopus smacked into her face and slipped into her mouth. Sprawling on twisting sea snakes, she tried to spit out the octopus – but it clung on, a tentacle twisting round her lip-ring. Its blue markings pulsed – the sign it was about to bite. With a blood-curdling shriek, she felt its deadly venom pump into her tongue. While she froze rigid, Maddie and Liz ran – just as Jez cut the rope holding Tyler's ankles.

With only time for a 'yikes', Tyler plunged into the seething red water below.

SEVEN

The purple speedboat choked into life as Liz fumbled at the controls.

'I've never driven one of these before,' she shouted over the engine's sudden roar. 'Hold tight for a rough ride!'

'It's got a radio, so I'll call the police,' Maddie called, just as Blake jumped in the back, yelling as he landed with a thud, 'As soon as I untie the rope, give her full blast.'

Liz turned to him. 'But where's your brother?'

'He's on his way.' Blake pointed to Tyler, running flat-out down the jetty – with Jez and Riki hot on his heels. 'As soon as Tyler jumps, give it full throttle.'

With bare feet pounding the planks, Tyler shrieked as he leapt off the jetty towards the boat.

He hurtled into the speedboat as it shot forward. Still drenched and gasping for breath, he sprawled on the deck as spray flew around them. Like a rocket, the boat soared over the water, slamming down into the waves and bouncing off them in bursts of white-out mist.

'Wow – that was close,' Tyler gulped. 'I thought I was done-for back there.'

'What kept you, mate?' Blake shouted above the screaming propellers, as the boat leapt from one giant wave to another, plunging through their crests in spewing showers of foam.

'Only a dirty great shark,' Tyler panted. 'It missed me by a centimetre. If I wasn't a swimming champ, it would have got me. And if Kirk wasn't so chunky, I'd be a goner. That shark had a gross mouthful … ' Suddenly he ducked as a shot ripped past him and splintered the dashboard, just missing Maddie who was shouting directions into the radio.

'The jet skis are gaining on us,' Blake shrieked. 'Get down!'

'Hold tighter,' Liz cried. 'A white-knuckle ride coming up. Time for zigzags … '

The boat swerved across the water with the jet skis close behind, bouncing wildly over their choppy wash. Wrenching the steering wheel first one way then another, Liz clung on for dear life as they criss-crossed the waves in a roaring blur.

Maddie picked up an oar and bawled, 'This might stop them.' She hurled it from the back of the speedboat and it smacked into the waves, just seconds before Jez slammed into it. He had no time to swerve and his jet ski struck it with a crack. Both he and his machine flew in a spluttering somersault. They plunged upside down in front of Riki, who smashed into them in an explosion of spray and crashing metal. Smoke and steam swirled from the bubbling sea.

With perfect timing, a police helicopter swept into view. The purple speedboat slowed and began to circle the sinking jet skis. Its engine chugged and purred as its passengers peered overboard for any sign of movement underwater.

'I reckon I've got the hang of this powerboat stuff now,' Liz laughed.

Maddie cheered, 'You were great. You've all been great. It's suddenly gone very quiet. Do you reckon those bad guys are DITW?'

'Not so much Dead In The Water as *Dumped* In The Water,' Blake beamed.

They saw two heads bob to the surface, then thrashing limbs followed by a splutter of obscenities.

'Mind your language, you guys – you'll attract the sharks!' Blake jeered.

'They'll soon get dragged out and arrested.' Liz pointed at a police dinghy racing towards them. 'Now it looks like a definite case of *Defeated* In The Water!'

'In fact,' Tyler added after great thought, 'I would say it's not so much DITW as WDIT.' He waited for them to respond.

'WDIT?'

'Sure,' he chuckled, '*We Did It. Together!*'

The dinghy drew up alongside them as the helicopter hovered above their jubilant high-fives.

'French fries kill more people than guns and sharks, yet nobody's afraid of French fries.'

Robert Kiyosaki

GIANT CLAMS

Giant clams are large shellfish (molluscs) that have two shells hinged together. The largest clams grow to more than 1.2 metres long. Once a giant clam settles into a place and begins to grow, it stays permanently attached to that spot for life – which could be for more than 100 years.

People used to believe that giant clams catch divers by quickly closing their shell and trapping the divers' hands or feet. This is something of a myth!

The Pearl of Lao Tzu is the largest known pearl in the world. It came from a giant clam in the Philippines. This famous clam pearl measures 24 centimetres in diameter and weighs 6.4 kilograms. That's a bit too big for a necklace!

BLUE-RINGED OCTOPUS

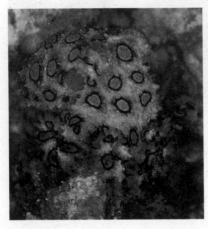

'Blue-rings' live in shallow coastal areas in Australia. There have been many reports of swimmers being bitten – and there have been several deaths. Often the victim is unaware of the danger and picks up or touches the small octopus (they are only 12 - 16 cm in size).

'Blue-rings' have even been known to bite through a wet suit, but the victim rarely feels anything – at first. Depending on how much venom is injected into the

wound, the effects of a blue-ringed octopus bite are quick. In five to ten minutes, the victim begins to feel numb, weak and has difficulty breathing and swallowing. Nausea and vomiting, blurred vision and difficulty speaking may follow. In severe cases, this is followed by paralysis, respiratory failure and unconsciousness.

Some victims have reported being conscious but unable to speak or move. Blue-ringed octopus venom is among the most toxic in the ocean.

MEGALODON

The megaldon shark was the biggest shark on Earth. Some of the teeth discovered from this largest of ocean predators have been as much as 17cm long. Megalodon was about three times the size of a great white shark and weighed about 48 metric tons – equal to as many as sixteen adult male African elephants. It could prey on anything and everything!

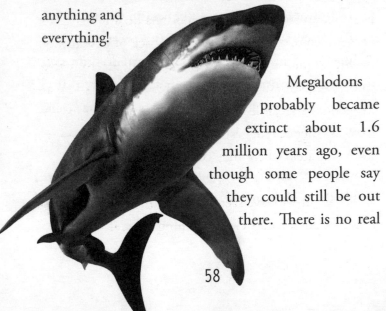

Megalodons probably became extinct about 1.6 million years ago, even though some people say they could still be out there. There is no real

evidence to suggest that megalodons do still exist. Yet an absence of evidence is not evidence of absence. So maybe some survived? It's very difficult to prove something doesn't exist, but that doesn't mean megalodons are still lurking in the deepest oceans. As fossil evidence suggests, they preferred shallower, warmer waters where they could hunt large prey.

So might we have seen them in the warm waters of the Australian coast? Go swimming there if you dare!

Now read the first chapter of another gripping adventure by John Townsend:

PERIL

IN THE SNOW

ONE

They came in the night without warning. Running footsteps in the moonlight … then the dreaded smashing of doors and the roar of flames.

No one was safe.

It was Hari's tenth birthday when The Night Raiders first struck. He was lucky that time. He woke in the night and saw red smoke rising from the next village.

There was just enough time for his family to grab

some things and run to the forest. It was better to risk the tigers than face robbers from the mountains.

*

The next year was different. The Night Raiders struck at the start of winter, under a moonless sky. The first Hari knew they were back was when he heard his sister scream just after midnight. He fled from his bed and ran out into the night just as the flames took hold.

For hours he hid in the hollow of a tree, with running footsteps all around in the smoke. He could only shiver in the snowy darkness until the screams finally fell silent.

In the first light of dawn, Hari stared in horror at where his home had been. All that remained were smouldering ashes in the snow. His parents and sister were nowhere to be seen.

He could only cling to the hope that they, like him, had hidden in the trees. But as the sun rose above the smoky treetops, he knew they had gone. Only later did he learn the terrible truth.

An old woman from the village told Hari what she had seen. His parents, she said sadly, had not survived the attack. His sister had been dragged away into the night. She was carried off into the mountains to become a slave of the dreaded Night Raiders.

'You will never see her again,' she wept.

John Townsend has been writing all sorts since he was a child – and he says he still hasn't grown up! John writes both fiction stories and non-fiction, and he loves writing for people who don't think they like books. (He always surprises them!)

John used to be a teacher, but now writes full-time. He is a recognised National Literacy Trust 'Reading Champion'.